WATCH OUT
FOR DINOSAURS!

The Nic-Nacs
and The Nic-Nac News

WATCH OUT
FOR DINOSAURS!

Joan Lowery Nixon

Illustrated by Toni Goffe

A YEARLING BOOK

Published by
Dell Publishing
a division of
Bantam Doubleday Dell Publishing Group, Inc.
666 Fifth Avenue
New York, New York 10103

ISBN: 0-440-40459-2

Printed in the United States of America

May 1991

10 9 8 7 6 5 4 3 2 1

OPM

For my grandson
Brian James Quinlan
with love

THE NIC-NAC NEWS

September 15   Issue #2
Reporters: Nicole Kimble, Nelson Slappey,
Amy Byrd, and Carlos Garza

PET DAY AT HONEYCUTT PARK

by Carlos Garza

All the kids in the neighborhood of Honeycutt Park are invited by the new Weekend Park Director Pete Erwin to bring their pets to a Pet Day. The day is next Saturday. The time is 2 p.m. There will be a pet parade and lots of prizes. If your pet can do tricks, this is its chance to be famous!

Please keep all dogs on leashes.

MYSTERIOUS DISAPPEARANCES AT PARK

by Nelson Slappey

A key to the pool storage cabinet mysteriously disappeared last Friday. Pete Erwin, Honeycutt Park director, claims that he put the key on a table near the cabinet. When he turned around the key was gone. Although the gate was unlocked, Mr. Erwin was the only one in the pool area.

A ring, one earring, and a dime also disappeared during the summer. Is the Honeycutt Park pool haunted? The only way we'll know for sure is if this mystery can be solved.

A POEM

by Amy Byrd

Who Says Rain Pitter-Patters?

Sometimes I've heard rain patter on the sidewalk,
and I've heard it whisper through the air,
and swoosh down the window glass,
and rattle inside the drainpipe
and gurgle in the gutters.
But I've never heard it pitter.
Has anybody?

PETITION FOR STOPLIGHT
ON FULLER AVENUE

by Nicole Kimble

During the past six months there have been six minor accidents and one serious accident at the corner of Fuller Avenue and Westheimer in our neighborhood. A stoplight is needed at this intersection.

Mr. Justin Wallace, who lives at 3418 Honeycutt Street, thinks that a petition, signed by as many neighbors as possible, will convince officials in the city's traffic department that a stoplight should be installed.

MR. WHAT'S WHAT

by Nelson Slappey

Question: When my cat wants to be fed she nips my leg, and it hurts. What should I do? (A.B., Houston)
Answer: Try saying "ouch!"

Question: How was the *Nanotyrannus* dinosaur like the *Tyrannosaurus Rex*? (C.G., Houston)
Answer: The skulls of both have wide foreheads, and the eye sockets face forward. The skulls are the same shape, but the skull of the *Nanotyrannus* is smaller. *Tyrannosaurus Rex* was about 18 feet tall and weighed 12,000 to 14,000 pounds. In comparison, the *Nanotyrannus* was about 10 feet tall and weighed only 600 to 1,000 pounds. They both had small front legs, walked on their hind legs, and ate meat.

CLASSIFIED ADS

Jamie Kimble, age 13, wants pet-sitting or baby-sitting jobs. Pets preferred. References. 555-2468.

Will mow & edge lawns, rake leaves, weed. Reasonable rates. Call Jeff Allen at 555-1073.

Ads free to anyone on Honeycutt Street.

1

Nelson Slappey kept his eyes on the magazine story he was reading as he reached for his orange juice and opened his mouth to take a drink.

"Slap! Watch what you're doing!" his mother said.

"Huh?" Slap put down his magazine and looked at the sugar bowl he was holding in his right hand. "Oh," he said. "I thought it was my orange juice."

Slap's big brother, Chris, who was hunched over his cereal bowl, grinned and made a snickering, snorting noise into his Krunchy Krackles.

"You can't read and eat at the same time," Slap's father said. "Whatever you're reading can wait until *after* breakfast."

"But I'm reading about dinosaurs," Slap said. "And it's important stuff."

Chris grabbed the sports section of the morning newspaper and threw it at Slap. "If you want to read something important, read this," he said.

"Oh, grasshopper guts!" Slap mumbled as the newspaper hit the side of his head. He threw it on the floor. All Chris thought about was sports. All he wanted to do was play football and basketball and baseball. Yuck.

And soccer. Another yuck.

Chris wasn't the least bit interested in science, but Slap was. Science was Slap's favorite subject in school. Last year he had been the only one in his class who had made a volcano that really smoked.

Ever since his class took a field trip to the Houston science museum and Slap saw the giant skeleton of a real *Diplodocus,* he especially wanted to read about dinosaurs. No matter what Chris said, dinosaurs were important.

Slap held up his magazine so everyone in his family could see it.

On the right side of the open pages was a drawing of a bird's skeleton on top of a drawing of the skeleton of a tyrannus dinosaur.

"Some scientists think that dinosaurs didn't die out," Slap said. "Did you know that the bones of birds are like the bones of the *Nanotyrannus* dinosaur?"

"Is that ugly thing supposed to be a dinosaur?" Chris asked as he pointed to the photograph on the left-hand side. The giant lizard in the picture was baring his sharp teeth.

"That's a different article," Slap said. "That's a Komodo dragon. It's not a dinosaur."

"It looks like a dinosaur," Chris said. "How big is that thing anyway?"

"Komodo dragons are usually ten feet long," Slap answered, "but they're not dinosaurs. They're lizards, and they live on some islands in the Indian Ocean."

"Lizards are reptiles, and so were some dinosaurs," Chris said.

"Stop talking about Komodo dragons!" Slap yelled at his brother. "I'm trying to tell everybody what I read about birds!"

"Those dragons look more like dinosaurs than your stupid birds do," Chris said.

It was true. They did. Slap glared at Chris. He hated it when Chris was right. "Yeah? Well, I'd like to put you on an island with a Komodo dragon. They eat fresh meat, just like *Tyrannosaurus Rex* did. A dragon would pick you up in his sharp teeth and crunch, munch—"

His mother shuddered. "Not at the table, please!" she said.

"Okay, Mom," Slap said. "I didn't want to talk about Komodo dragons anyway. I wanted to tell you about how some scientists think that birds are related to dinosaurs. That means—"

His mother interrupted. "Everything you've told us is interesting," she said, "but it's almost time for you to leave for school, and you haven't eaten your cereal."

Slap took a big bite. Some milk ran down his chin, so he wiped his chin on the back of his hand. He tried to go back to reading his magazine article, but his father took the magazine out of his hand and set it aside.

"Hurry up, Slap," his father said. "You can't be late for school."

Slap took an even bigger bite. He knew he

wasn't supposed to talk while his mouth was full, but his mother and father didn't understand. "Don't you see?" Slap said. "This is big news! If the scientists are right, then dinosaurs aren't extinct."

Chris jumped up from the table, his fingers curled like sharp claws. He growled at Slap and said, "I'm a Komodo dragon, and I'm coming to get you!"

As Chris lunged, Slap ducked, spilling his orange juice.

"Oh, dear. Not again," Slap's mother said.

Slap's father mopped up the juice with paper towels and poured more orange juice in Slap's glass. "Down the hatch," he told Slap. "If you want to make the junior soccer team next year, you'll need to put some meat on your bones."

Slap gulped the orange juice until it was gone, then wiped his mouth on the back of his hand. He didn't want to make the junior soccer team next year or any year.

"Tomorrow's Saturday, so we'll try to find time to get in a little practice," Slap's father told him. "Chris can help you too."

Slap knew that sports were important to his father because he was a P.E. teacher and bas-

ketball coach at Porter Junior High, but sports weren't at all important to Slap. "I'd rather read about dinosaurs," Slap said, but nobody seemed to hear him.

A few minutes later Carlos Garza, Slap's best friend and next-door neighbor, came by to walk to school with Slap. Just ahead of them were Nikki Kimble and Amy Byrd, the other two Nic-Nacs. *Nic* for Nicole, *N* for Nelson, *A* for Amy, and *C* for Carlos. *Nic-Nacs*. Slap liked being one of the Nic-Nacs.

Sometimes when Nikki and Amy saw Carlos and Slap, they walked faster, trying to get to school first, but this time they turned and waited for them to catch up.

Nikki said, "Right after school we have to go to Honeycutt Park."

"Why?" Slap asked.

"Mr. Erwin called Mom," she said. "He asked her if we could come to the park after school because he has some news for our newspaper."

"Who's Mr. Erwin?" Carlos asked.

Amy said, "He's the new playground director for Honeycutt Park."

"Did he say what his news is?" Slap asked.

Nikki brushed her hair out of her eyes. "Not

exactly," she said. "All I know is that it's something he's planning to do for the kids who come to the park. He did tell Mom something strange, though."

The others stopped and looked at her. "What did he say that was strange?" Amy asked.

"He said that some things around the swimming pool had disappeared—the key to the pool storage cabinet, for one thing."

"Does he think someone took it?" Carlos asked.

"Mr. Erwin doesn't know how it happened because he thinks he was the only one there when it disappeared."

Slap gave a wicked chuckle. "Maybe the storage cabinet is haunted."

"Don't do that!" Nikki said. "I hate it when you try to scare us." She began walking toward school again, and the others hurried to catch up.

"Why would anyone want the key?" Carlos asked. "The pool's only open on weekends now and will be closed all the time after September."

"Another mystery," Slap said in a deep raspy voice.

Nikki glared at Slap. "It's not a mystery," she said. "It's just a missing key."

"But you said some other things were missing too," Slap told her.

Nikki shrugged. "Okay. The lifeguard had written a report about some stuff that disappeared during the summer."

"Aha!" Slap said.

"What disappeared?" Amy asked.

"I don't remember all of it," Nikki said.

"If you were a good reporter you'd remember," Slap told her.

Nikki's cheeks turned pink. "I do remember one thing," she said. "Mrs. Bartlett had left a small gold-colored ring on one of the tables while she went swimming, and when she got back a few minutes later it was gone."

"That's terrible," Amy said.

Nikki shook her head. "Mrs. Bartlett said it was just costume jewelry and wasn't valuable."

"I mean it's terrible that somebody took it. Did Mrs. Bartlett see anyone near the table?"

"No," Nikki said. "During the summer she went swimming as soon as the pool opened every morning. Except for the lifeguard, she was sometimes the only one at the pool."

"The haunted swimming pool," Slap said in a low scary voice.

"The ring probably just rolled off the table," Carlos said.

"Then sooner or later someone would have found it," Slap said. "I think we really do have a mystery." This time he gave a deep cackling laugh.

Nikki turned to face him. "Instead of making scary noises, why don't you solve the mystery?"

"Maybe I will," Slap said.

A leaf fell from an overhead branch, hitting Slap on the nose. He jumped up and slapped the branch, shaking the tree.

Four large black crows flapped up from the tree with loud complaints. One sailed over to a nearby lawn and began hunting for bugs in the grass, but one scolded Slap before it swooped to the top of another tree.

"Caw, caw!" Slap yelled back at it.

Carlos ran in a circle around the other Nic-Nacs. He startled a squirrel, which dropped a shiny gum wrapper it was holding and dashed across the street.

"It would have tasted terrible," Slap told the squirrel.

Carlos jumped over a small bush and then a larger one. "I know what news story Mr. Erwin is going to give us," he said. "Every year we have a Sports Day, so I bet he's planning a Sports Day."

Slap groaned. He hated Sports Day.

"I hope that's what the news is," Carlos said. "Sports Day is great. There are always races, and a baseball game, and a broad jump."

"And volleyball," Amy said. "That's my favorite."

"Tony likes Sports Day," Carlos said. "He likes to watch everyone play, and it makes him happy if I play catch with him."

Tony—Antonio—was Carlos's little brother. Slap liked Tony. Everybody liked Tony. Mrs. Garza called Tony a special child, and he went to a school just for children who couldn't learn the way other children did.

"If they're going to have sack races again, I'm going to start practicing right now," Nikki said. She laughed. "I love Sports Day."

Slap didn't want to think about Sports Day. He knew that Chris would play in the baseball game, and their father would wear his old baseball cap and cheer for Chris. And he'd tell

Slap, "I know you weren't cut out for Little League, but next year you'll be eligible for the neighborhood team. We'll have to work hard to get you in shape."

"Grasshopper guts!" Slap said.

"Yuck!" Amy said.

"What's the matter with you?" Nikki asked him.

"Grasshopper guts," Slap said again. "Purple and green squishy grasshopper guts!" He didn't want to talk anymore about Sports Day. "Race you!" he yelled, and ran toward the front gates of Albertson Elementary School.

As always, when they raced, Carlos passed him and got there first.

2

Slap had brought his magazine to school. He showed the article about dinosaurs to Mrs. Lambkin. "I could write a science report about this," he said.

Mrs. Lambkin picked up a stack of papers and walked to the window side of the room. "That's a good idea," she said. "We'll begin writing science reports the first part of next month."

Slap followed her. He didn't want to wait until next month. "I can tell you about the dinosaurs now," he said.

"We don't have time now," Mrs. Lambkin said. "The tardy bell will ring in just about two minutes." She handed half of the papers to Slap. "Why don't you help me pass these out?"

Slap looked at the papers. They were the math tests they'd taken on Monday. Fractions. Slap was having trouble with fractions. He was afraid of what his grade would be.

"I'll help! Let me!" Chrissy Sue jumped out of her seat and ran to the front of the room. The pink bow on her curly blond hair bounced as she ran.

"Thank you," Mrs. Lambkin said. She gave Chrissy Sue the rest of the papers.

Chrissy Sue scurried around the room, handing out her share of the papers and looking important. Slap tucked his magazine safely inside his notebook, then began distributing the test papers Mrs. Lambkin had given him.

As the tardy bell rang, Chrissy Sue jerked the rest of the papers out of Slap's hands. "I finished already, slowpoke," she said. "I'll hand out yours."

Before Slap could stop her she said loudly, "I put your paper on your desk. You got a C-minus." She smiled. "I got an A."

Everyone was looking, and Slap could feel his face turn red. "Oh, grasshopper guts," he said.

Chrissy Sue wrinkled her nose. "Yuck! You're disgusting!" she said.

"Thank you," Slap said. He slumped in his seat. He wished he had a Komodo dragon. He'd let it eat Chrissy Sue.

Nikki leaned across the aisle and whispered to Slap, "Don't mind her."

Carlos looked in Chrissy Sue's direction and made a stuck-up face, and Amy held up her paper so Slap could see that she had got a C too. Slap felt much better.

After school Slap dropped his books at home and gulped down two chocolate chip cookies and a glass of milk.

His mother sat beside Slap and asked, "How was school today?"

Slap thought about the C-minus on his arithmetic paper. He didn't want to talk about school. "I have to go to the park now with Carlos and Nikki and Amy," he said.

His mother gave him a quick kiss. "Be careful crossing the streets," she said.

He ran all the way to Nikki's house to meet the other Nic-Nacs in the Kimbles' kitchen.

Nikki brushed her hair out of her eyes,

picked up her pencil, and looked at it. "Who's got a pencil with a point on it?" she asked.

"I do," Carlos said. He pulled a stubby pencil out of the pocket of his jeans.

"Then you get to write the news story," Nikki said. She handed him a small lined notepad.

"Mom!" she shouted. "We're going to walk to the park now. Okay?"

Mrs. Kimble came into the kitchen. She took a barrette out of a jar on the windowsill and put it in Nikki's hair. "Okay," she said, "but be careful crossing the streets."

Slap knew she would say that. Mothers always said that.

Nikki's little sister, Mandy, crawled out from under the table. "I want to go too," she said.

Nikki groaned. "Aw, Mom!" she said.

"Not this time," Mrs. Kimble told Mandy. "The park is four blocks away. Your legs would get tired."

Mandy looked at Slap and held up her arms. "Carry me," she said.

"I can't," Slap said. "Look at my arms. No bones." He dangled his arms and let them wobble so it looked as if the bones had fallen out.

"Next time, Mandy," Mrs. Kimble said.

Mandy looked so unhappy that Slap felt mean, but he was glad that Mandy wasn't coming with them. Little sisters were pests. So were big brothers.

On the way to Honeycutt Park Carlos talked about last year's Sports Day, but Slap didn't listen. He thought about Komodo dragons instead.

He wished there was a Komodo dragon in the Houston zoo so he could see a real live one, but as far as he knew there wasn't a zoo in the whole world that had a Komodo dragon.

The Nic-Nacs turned into Honeycutt Park and walked past the tennis courts and playground. Beyond the playground was the field for baseball games. Inside a high, locked chain-link fence was the swimming pool, and next to the swimming pool was the office.

The surface of the water in the pool suddenly rippled, the way it did when someone was swimming under water. But no one was there.

The breeze did it, Slap thought to himself. But it was still hot weather, and there wasn't much of a breeze. Haunted swimming pool?

Slap was scaring himself. He quickly looked away.

A squirrel ran across the grass and scampered up one of the trees near the pool. A pair of the large black crows that built their nests in that tree each year angrily scolded the squirrel and flew to another tree.

A young man with a sunburned nose and sunbleached hair opened the office door and called out to them. "Hi!" he said. "I'm Pete Erwin."

"Hi, Mr. Erwin," Nikki said. "We're the Nic-Nacs." She introduced all of them.

"Why don't you just call me Pete?" Mr. Erwin said. "Come on into my office. As I told Mrs. Kimble, I've got some news for your neighborhood newspaper."

"Are you going to tell us about the mystery too?" Slap asked.

"You mean the missing key?" Pete shrugged. "All I know is that I put it down on one of the outdoor tables. I stacked some of the lawn chairs and put them in the storage cabinet. I turned around to get the key to lock the cabinet, and the key was gone."

"And you were the only one there at the time, weren't you?" Nikki said.

"As far as I know."

"What about the other things that disappeared?" Slap asked.

Pete took a half-dozen papers from the top desk drawer and handed them to Slap. "Here are the lifeguard's reports. The missing items included a gold-colored ring, one gold earring, a dime, a few other odd things like that. You figure it out."

"That's what Slap's going to do," Nikki said. "He's going to solve your mystery." She gave Slap a wicked smile.

"Yeah. Maybe I will," Slap said. He wished Nikki hadn't said that. How was he going to solve a strange mystery like this one?

"Everybody sit down," Pete said. "I'll tell you what I have in mind."

As soon as they'd all taken chairs, Carlos asked, "Are we going to have a Sports Day?"

"Sports Day?" Pete repeated. He looked surprised. "Maybe later. Right now I've got something else in mind. That's why I called you."

Carlos took his pencil and notepad from his pocket. "What is it?" he asked.

Pete reached under the desk and pulled out some posters. "I made these to advertise Pet Day," he said. "I'm going to put them up at the grocery store and the drugstore and here at the park. A week from tomorrow at three o'clock all the kids in the neighborhood can bring their pets here to the park."

"What will we do with our pets?" Amy asked.

"First, they'll be in a parade," Pete answered. "If the pets know any tricks they can do them too."

Carlos wrote down everything Pete was saying.

"There's one important rule," Pete told Carlos. "Dogs will have to stay on their leashes." He smiled. "We'll have lots of awards. I'm making a list—smallest pet, biggest dog, fluffiest cat."

"I'll bring our cat!" Amy said.

"Cinderella isn't fluffy," Nikki said.

"But she's pretty," Amy said. "She has one blue eye and one green eye."

"We may have an award for cats like that," Pete said.

"My aunt Eileen gave me a turtle," Nikki

said. "I named him Speedy. He'd be perfect to bring to Pet Day."

"I'll bring Izzy," Carlos said.

"Who's Izzy?" Pete asked.

"Izzy's my dog," Carlos said. "When he was a puppy he got into everything, and my mom kept asking, 'Where is he? Where is he?' So we named him Izzy."

Everyone but Slap laughed.

Slap didn't feel like laughing. More than anything else he wanted a dog, but he didn't have one. If he couldn't have a dog, he'd like a cat, or any kind of a pet at all. He could ask his mom again if she'd let him have a pet, but it wouldn't do any good. He knew it. She'd just say no again.

"Oh, grasshopper guts!" he mumbled to himself.

3

When the Nic-Nacs met at Nikki's house the next morning, Mrs. Kimble was working at her computer.

"What are you writing? Is it a short story?" Slap asked her. He leaned over her shoulder.

"It's an interview article," she said. "I interviewed four people who work with community theaters in Houston to get their ideas about local theater."

"Are any of the people famous?" Amy asked.

Mrs. Kimble looked surprised. "They're well known in Houston," she said.

"I would love to interview somebody *really* famous," Amy said. "Like a movie star."

"You'll have to wait until you're grown up," Slap told her. "Famous people don't let kids interview them."

Mrs. Kimble suddenly hopped out of her chair. "Oh!" she said. "I have a message for all of you. Mr. Wallace telephoned. He wants your help."

"What does he want us to do?" Nikki asked.

Her mother said, "He's written a petition asking the city to put a stoplight on Fuller Avenue. There have been a number of accidents there because there's no stoplight, so he hopes that in the next issue of *The Nic-Nac News* you'll write about the petition and urge the neighbors to sign it."

She handed her notes to Nikki.

"Thanks," Nikki said. "We'll write a story about it."

"Before you do, you should telephone Mr. Wallace," Mrs. Kimble told her.

"Why? You wrote down everything he told you," Nikki said.

"A good reporter always goes right to the source and double-checks facts," her mother said. "Your uncle Bill taught me that."

"Okay," Nikki said. She picked up the kitchen

telephone and dialed the phone number her mother had printed.

While Nikki talked to Mr. Wallace, the other Nic-Nacs sat at the kitchen table. Mrs. Kimble had put some freshly sharpened pencils and some paper on the table.

She poured apple juice for all of them and put a plate of Oreo cookies on the table too.

Nikki finished her telephone call and sat at the table. Each of the Nic-Nacs reached for a cookie. They pulled the two halves apart and ate the frosting in the middle first. Mrs. Kimble took a cookie and bit right into it. *That was a strange way to eat an Oreo*, Slap thought.

"I'll write about Mr. Wallace's petition," Nikki said.

"I'll write about Pet Day," Carlos said.

"I'll write about the mystery," Slap said.

"I'll write a poem," Amy said.

They all looked at her.

"A poem isn't a news story," Carlos said.

"Newspapers have more than news stories in them," Amy said. "There's no reason they can't have poems. I want to write a poem."

Slap said, "Roses are red, violets are blue."

Carlos joined in, "I know a frog who looks like you."

Slap and Carlos laughed and hooted, but Amy said, "You're not funny."

Nikki didn't laugh either. "Go ahead, Amy," she said. "Write a poem. You write good poems."

"But a poem isn't news," Slap complained.

Mrs. Kimble said, "A newspaper has many things in it besides news stories. Some of them are called *features*."

"Like crossword puzzles?" Carlos asked.

"Yes. They're features," Mrs. Kimble answered. "And so are advice columns and book reviews."

"And movie and television reviews!" Amy said. "And interviews with famous people."

"I guess my 'Mr. What's What' column is a feature," Slap said.

Nikki looked at him. "Did anyone send you a question for your column?"

Slap shook his head.

"How can you write a question-and-answer column if you don't get any questions?"

"Do you know how the *Nanotyrannus* dinosaur was like the *Tyrannosaurus Rex*?" Slap asked.

"No," Carlos said. "How?"

"Thanks," Slap said. "Now I've got a question."

Any laughed. "I've got another question for you," she said. She wrote it and handed the paper to Slap.

"I almost forgot," Nikki said. "Jamie gave us an ad for our newspaper."

Carlos pulled a scrap of paper from his pocket. "Jeff Allen asked if we were going to have ads. He gave me this. He wants the neighbors to know he'll mow lawns."

"Should we charge for ads?" Amy asked.

Slap thought about how hard it was to mow lawns in hot weather. "Why don't we make the ads free for anyone who lives on Honeycutt Street?" he asked.

The other Nic-Nacs agreed.

"We better start writing," Nikki said. "We want Mom to type and print our newspaper before lunch so we can deliver it this afternoon."

She asked her mother, "How do you spell Mr. Wallace's first name? Or are you going to tell me to call him up again?"

Her mother smiled. "Let me ask you a question first. How are you going to start your story?"

Nikki looked surprised. "Umm, 'Mr. Wallace has a petition he wants neighbors to sign.' Something like that."

"A good news story always begins with the most important fact," Mrs. Kimble said. "What's the most important fact in your story?"

Nikki thought a moment. "The need for the traffic light," she said.

Her mother smiled. "Good answer. Mr. Wallace's name isn't as important. That can come later, and his first name is spelled J-U-S-T-I-N."

Slap began writing. He remembered what he'd read about the *Nanotyrannus* dinosaur. He could spell *Nanotyrannus* and *Tyrannosaurus Rex* without any trouble. Those words were easy. The ones he got mixed up were *their* and *there* and *they're*, and *which* and *witch*. He answered Amy's question first, then answered the question about dinosaurs. He wished he had more space. There was lots he'd like to write about dinosaurs.

Next Slap wrote about the mystery at the park. It was such a strange mystery that he didn't see how he or anyone else could figure out the answer.

When everyone had finished writing, Mrs. Kimble corrected the words that were spelled wrong and sat down at her computer to type the news stories. "Your newspaper is wonderful," she said. "That Pet Day at the park sounds like fun."

Pet Day!

Slap had forgotten about Pet Day. He pushed back his chair. "I've got to go home right away," he said. "I'll come back this afternoon to help deliver the newspaper."

He needed to talk to his mom. Pet Day was in just one week, and he had to talk her into letting him get a pet. If he didn't have a pet, how could he go to Pet Day?

When he got home he found his mother reading a book. She put it down and smiled at Slap. "Is it time for lunch already?" she asked. "Your father and Chris should be back from the hardware store at any minute, so how about helping me make grilled cheese sandwiches for everyone?"

Slap followed his mother to the kitchen. "I have to talk to you," he said.

Mrs. Slappey stopped and looked at him. "What happened?" she asked.

"Nothing happened," Slap said, "but something's going to happen."

His mother sat on a kitchen stool. She put her hands on Slap's shoulders and looked into his eyes. "What's going to happen?" she asked.

Why did mothers worry so much? "It's nothing bad," Slap said. "That is, it could be bad, or it could be good. It's up to you."

His mother took a deep breath. "Slap," she said, "tell me right now. What's going to happen?"

"Pet Day," Slap said.

"What are we talking about?" Mrs. Slappey sighed.

Slap quickly told her about all the kids bringing their pets to Pet Day. "So I have to get a pet before Saturday," he explained. "Like a dog. I really want a dog."

"Oh, dear." His mother looked sad. "Slap," she said, "we can't have a dog right now."

"It doesn't have to be a big dog," Slap told her. "It can be a little dog."

She shook her head. "We're all at work or at

school during the day, and no one would be home to train a puppy."

"It doesn't have to be a puppy. It can be a grown dog."

"The dog would be lonesome and unhappy," Mrs. Slappey told him. "There'd be no one here to take care of him."

"I'll take care of him!" Slap promised. "I'll even run home from school during lunch period to play with him. And while you're driving clients around, trying to sell them houses, you could stop in just to say hello to the dog."

"I'm sorry, Slap," his mother said, "but we aren't going to get a dog."

Slap couldn't give up. "Then how about a cat?"

"No. Cats scratch the furniture."

"A fish?"

"Fish take a lot of care." She patted Slap's shoulder. "How about some lunch? You can have the first sandwich."

Slap didn't want to eat lunch.

He went outside and sat on the back steps. Over his head a squirrel leaped from one tree limb to another. It sat up and nibbled on something it held tightly in its paws while it watched Slap. Maybe he could trap a squirrel and put it in a cage and take it to Pet Day.

. The squirrel leaped to another branch and disappeared. *Not a squirrel*, Slap thought. The squirrel was happy and free, and it wouldn't be happy locked up in a cage.

A small green lizard ran up the tree trunk. It would be easy to catch a lizard. He could cut small holes in a shoe box and put the lizard inside.

The lizard turned brown and ran down the tree trunk, disappearing into the grass. No. The lizard would hate being in a shoe box.

Slap would have to think of something else. But what?

"Slap!" his mother called. "Carlos is here. He's going to have lunch with us."

Slap decided he did feel a little hungry. He joined Carlos in the kitchen, and they pulled out chairs at the table where Slap's father was already seated.

"Wash your hands first," Mrs. Slappey said. She glanced at Carlos's hands. "Both of you, please," she added.

Slap and Carlos washed their hands in the bathroom and headed back to the kitchen. But as Slap came near his open bedroom door, he heard a strange scratching noise and a low rumbling sound. He stopped and looked into his room. No one was there, but something caught his eye.

"Wait a minute," he said to Carlos. "I didn't leave my science magazine on the floor. Someone's been in my room." He walked into his bedroom, Carlos right behind him.

Slap listened. He thought he heard the faint scratching again. "Did you hear anything?" he asked Carlos.

They listened intently, but Slap didn't hear the sound again.

Carlos pointed to the floor and asked, "What are those?"

Slap saw the chalky footprints. They were huge three-toed footprints, and they led from the magazine to the closed door of his closet.

Slap, with Carlos right behind him, followed the footprints to his closet door.

A drippy slurping noise came from inside the closet.

"I heard *that*," Carlos said.

"What is it?" Slap whispered. "What's in my closet?"

"We won't know unless we open the door and look," Carlos said.

Slowly and cautiously Slap turned the knob and opened the door.

Slap let out a yell, and Carlos fell backward on the bed as a huge, dark dragon with sharp, pointed teeth gave an ear-splitting growl and rushed out of the closet!

4

"I'm a Komodo dragon!" Chris yelled. He ran around Slap's bedroom with a black-paper lizard head over his own.

"Cut it out!" Slap said.

"I scared you silly!" Chris shouted. He pulled off the paper lizard head and threw it at Slap.

Slap caught it and took a good look at it. It really wasn't a bad dragon head, but he wasn't going to tell Chris that. "You didn't need this thing," he said. "You look more like the Komodo dragon without it."

Carlos picked up the magazine and stared at the picture of the dragon. "What an ugly face!" he said.

"Yeah, but he's my brother, so we try to be nice to him," Slap said.

"Boys!" Mrs. Slappey yelled. "Come to lunch! Right now!"

Chris ran down the hall, laughing loudly.

As Slap put the dragon head on the shelf in his closet, Carlos grinned and said, "It really was kind of funny."

"Yeah," Slap said, "but don't tell Chris that."

As soon as lunch was over, Slap's father had to hurry to his school for basketball practice. Chris went with him, because he was on the team.

Slap helped his mother clear the table and put the dishes in the dishwasher. "Carlos and I have to help deliver *The Nic-Nac News*," he said as soon as they'd finished.

"Race you!" Carlos yelled, and they ran down the block to Nikki's house.

Carlos got there first, of course.

Slap and Carlos took the side of the street with the even numbers, and Amy and Nikki took the side with the odd numbers, and they began to deliver their newspapers.

This time Mrs. Flores didn't giggle. "I can't wait to read it," she said, and gave them a nickel.

This time Mrs. Wallace didn't say "Isn't that cute!" She said, "Oh, good. There's a news story about the stoplight." She gave them a nickel.

Mr. Sibley only said, "Hummph," but he gave them a dime.

Mrs. January read the headline about Pet Day. "That sounds like fun," she said. "I'd like to go and take my parakeet, Keetsy."

Slap and Carlos looked at each other. "It's only for kids," Slap said.

"I may look old on the outside," Mrs. January said, "but on the inside I'm still young." She smiled. "But it doesn't matter. We're going to be out of town that day."

Chrissy Sue Danby was in her front yard. She was playing with a furry white puppy with big black eyes. The puppy wiggled and bounced and ran right to Slap.

Slap wished he had a puppy just like this one. He smiled at the puppy, who wiggled and wagged its tail in response.

Slap bent to pick up the puppy, but Chrissy Sue got to it first.

"My grandmother gave me this puppy," Chrissy Sue said. "I named him Snuggles. Isn't

he beautiful?" She kissed the puppy on his nose.

Slap wished his grandmother would give him a puppy. He reached out to pet the puppy, but Chrissy Sue pulled Snuggles out of Slap's reach.

Slap frowned. "Grasshopper guts!" he said.

The puppy looked at Slap and whimpered.

Slap looked away. He felt terrible. He didn't mean to hurt the puppy's feelings.

Amy and Nikki crossed the street to join them. They made cooing noises at Snuggles, but Chrissy Sue wouldn't let them touch her puppy either.

"There's going to be a Pet Day at Honeycutt Park next Saturday," Amy told Chrissy Sue. "You could bring Snuggles. I'm going to bring my cat, Cinderella."

"I'm going to bring Speedy, my turtle," Nikki said.

"I'm going to bring my dog, Izzy," Carlos said.

Chrissy Sue looked at Slap.

Slap didn't say anything.

"Don't you have a pet?" she asked.

"No," Slap said.

Chrissy Sue hugged Snuggles and smiled. "Then ha-ha, you can't go to Pet Day," she said.

"Slap can go. He's going to help me with Izzy," Carlos said.

But Slap heard himself saying "I'm going to bring a pet."

Why had he said that? Where was he going to get a pet? Everyone was staring at him.

"What kind of a pet?" Chrissy Sue asked.

"Never mind," Slap mumbled.

Chrissy Sue laughed and said, "You already said you don't have a pet. Liar, liar! Pants on fire!"

"I am not a liar!" Slap said.

Chrissy Sue stared at him. "Then what's your pet?"

Slap took a deep breath and said the first thing that came into his head. "I'm going to bring a dinosaur. A real, live dinosaur!"

None of the Nic-Nacs said a word, but Chrissy Sue laughed so hard she threw herself on the ground.

Slap's face burned. He wanted to run away and hide. What was the matter with him? Why had he said that he'd bring a dinosaur? Where was he going to find a dinosaur?

"Liar, liar!" Chrissy Sue began again.

Carlos shoved a copy of *The Nic-Nac News* into her hand. "Here," he said. "Read about Pet Day in this."

As the Nic-Nacs walked back to Nikki's house, Slap could hear Chrissy Sue still laughing. He didn't know what he was going to do.

Carlos said, "Maybe you could use that dragon head that Chris made. It looks like a dinosaur. We could get more black paper and make a body for it."

Slap shook his head. "I said I'd bring a *live* dinosaur," he said.

"Mandy has dinosaur pajamas," Nikki said. "She could wear them and you could pretend it was all part of a joke."

Slap shook his head.

"I said I'd bring a *real* dinosaur," he told her.

"Chrissy Sue is going to tell everyone at school," Nikki said.

"So we'll have to think of *something*," Amy said.

"Before Saturday," Carlos said.

Slap frowned and told them, "I said I'd bring a real, live dinosaur, so I will."

"Where are you going to find a real, live dinosaur?" Nikki asked.

Slap wished he knew.

5

Slap walked home by himself, kicking at rocks and scuffing his shoes in the dirt. He stared down at the ground as he passed Mrs. January's house, even though he knew that Mrs. January was sitting on her front porch, rocking in her big rocking chair, with her parakeet, Keetsy, in his cage beside her, as usual.

Most of the time Slap liked to talk to Mrs. January, but he didn't feel like talking to anybody right now.

But when Mrs. January called to Slap, "Come and sit with me a minute," he slowly climbed the steps and plopped down on the top step.

Mrs. January didn't ask "What's the matter?"

or say "Why don't you tell me what's bothering you." She said, "Hello, Mr. What's What. I read what you wrote about the *Nanotyrannus* dinosaur. I'd like to know more about it."

Slap looked up, surprised. "You would?"

"Sure," Mrs. January said. "I like to read about dinosaurs. So tell me, where did they find out about this *Nanotyrannus* dinosaur? I never heard of him before."

"His skull was on a shelf in a Cleveland museum for years before anybody really studied it," Slap said. "Then along came three scientists who measured and tested it and decided it was really the skull of a *Nanotyrannus*."

As Slap told Mrs. January everything he couldn't find space for in his column, he grew more and more excited.

"My, my," Mrs. January said. "You really are a Mr. What's What. You know so many interesting things."

Keetsy began to preen himself. Slap poked a finger into Keetsy's cage, and Keetsy carefully stepped onto it.

"He likes me," Slap said.

Nikki ran out of her front door and across her yard to Mrs. January's house.

"Hello, Mrs. January," she said.

"Hello, Nikki," Mrs. January answered. "Come on up here on the porch. Slap's been telling me some interesting things."

Nikki shook her head. "I can't. I just came to tell Slap that Carlos and Amy and I are going swimming, and we want him to go too."

"Okay," Slap said. The idea of cool water on a hot day sounded good.

"Before you go, Slap, I'd like to ask you to do me a favor," Mrs. January said. "Tomorrow we're going to visit relatives in Austin and will be gone for two weeks. My friend who was going to take care of Keetsy just called to tell me she can't do it after all, and I've been trying to get hold of another friend who hasn't called back. How about you? Could you take care of Keetsy for me while we're gone?"

"Sure!" Slap grinned at the bird. "I'll take good care of you, Keetsy."

"Thank you," Mrs. January said. "He'll be your pet while I'm away from home." She fished a door key from her skirt pocket and handed it to Slap as she told him how to care for her parakeet.

Slap said good-bye to Mrs. January, but as he

walked down the porch steps she said, "I hope you keep writing that 'Mr. What's What' column. I like to read it."

Nikki walked with Slap to the sidewalk. She looked excited, as if she knew something that he didn't know. "I've been thinking about those things that disappeared from near the swimming pool," she said. "None of them was valuable."

"I know," Slap said. "Who'd want a key, a ring, one earring, and a dime?"

Nikki's eyes were bright. "I think I know who would! I figured it out!"

"Who?" Slap asked.

"Didn't you ever play treasure hunt?" Nikki asked. "Everybody has to find a list of odd things, and the winner is the one who brings them back to the party first."

"That would be an awfully long party," Slap said.

Nikki shrugged. "There has to be some reason why someone is taking them. I thought if we could come up with a reason, we could figure out who the thief is."

Slap thought a moment. "Maybe we should set a trap," he said.

Nikki looked interested. "What kind of trap?"

"I don't know. Maybe put something else on one of the tables by the pool and then hide and watch and see if someone comes to take it." He shrugged. "I don't know if the trap would work. I don't even know what to put in the trap."

"I do!" Nikki told him. "I've got a fake emerald ring I won in the fishpond booth at the last school carnival. We can use that."

"Maybe we really will solve the mystery," Slap said. He smiled at Nikki, and she smiled back.

"Hurry up and get your swim suit on," Nikki told him. "I'll bring the ring, and we'll see what happens."

Slap walked home with his head up. He felt a lot better. The leaves of a Chinese tallow tree were turning gold and red, and a squirrel bounced across his path, stopping to snatch up an acorn. A crow swooped so close to the squirrel's head that the squirrel ducked and ran up the trunk of the nearest tree to hide. Slap laughed aloud.

As he passed Chrissy Sue's house he made a face. He didn't care that Chrissy Sue had laughed at him. He wouldn't care if she told everybody at school he was going to bring a dinosaur to Pet Day. He wouldn't even care if *everybody* laughed.

For a moment his stomach hurt. Of course he'd care.

He reminded himself that at least he could go to Pet Day with a pet, since Mrs. January had said that Keetsy would be his pet while she was away from home. But he'd look so dumb if he brought a parakeet when he'd told everyone he'd bring a dinosaur. No. Somehow he'd have to come up with a dinosaur.

When he got home, Slap put Mrs. January's door key in his top dresser drawer. He hurried into his swim suit, pulled an old T-shirt over his head, and grabbed a towel. Then he ran all the way to Nikki's house, where he met the other Nic-Nacs. Nikki had already told them the plan, so all of them were excited when they reached the park.

Because the pool would be open only two more weekends, the area was crowded. Many of the tables were piled with towels and diaper bags and soft-drink coolers.

"Over there," Carlos said, pointing to a table

away from the others. "There's nothing on that table."

Nikki tugged the ring from the pocket of her shorts and carefully placed it in the center of the table. Its green glass caught the sunlight.

"Perfect," Amy whispered.

"Let's walk away slowly," Slap said from one corner of his mouth. "Pretend we had nothing to do with the ring. We'll dump our stuff on the grass under the tree."

"We'll take turns swimming," Nikki said. "Somebody will have to keep an eye on the ring."

They all had fun in the water, and they all took turns watching over the ring. It glittered in the sunlight, but no one seemed to notice it or come near it.

It was Slap's turn again to stand guard when he saw Chrissy Sue's family arriving at the pool. Chrissy Sue had a bright red-and-orange ruffled bathing suit with a jacket and flip-flops to match. "Ugh!" Slap said to himself.

From the corners of his eyes he watched Chrissy Sue and her family as they passed the table with the ring on it. Chrissy Sue suddenly stopped as she spotted the ring, and her brother, Jack, tripped over her.

"Watch where you're going!" he complained as he picked himself up.

Slap scrunched down and slid halfway behind the tree, hoping that Chrissy Sue wouldn't see him.

Her family put their things on two lawn chairs and splashed into the water, but Chrissy Sue sneaked back to the table, picked up the ring, and tried it on.

She cautiously glanced around, to the right and to the left, and suddenly looked directly at Slap. Quickly she put down the ring, ran to the pool, and jumped into the water.

Grasshopper guts! Would Chrissy Sue have taken the ring if she hadn't seen Slap watching her? Or was she just curious and would have put it down anyway? Slap didn't know.

When the others came out of the pool, he told them about Chrissy Sue.

Amy shook her head. "I think she was just looking," she said. "Don't forget, no one was around when all those things were taken. If Chrissy Sue had been here, someone would have seen her."

"That's what's wrong with our plan," Nikki said. "We should have thought of that. We'll have to come back when the pool's open and not many people will be here."

"Sunday night," Carlos and Slap said together. "The pool's open until nine, but most people go home as soon as it gets dark."

"Then we'll all come tomorrow night," Nikki said. She dropped the ring into the pocket of her shorts, and the Nic-Nacs headed for home.

After dinner Carlos came over, and he and Slap played in Slap's room with his model cars until they got bored. Slap got out the Komodo dragon head, and they took turns putting it on and growling at each other.

"It's too bad the Pet Day isn't after dark," Carlos said. "We could make a body to go with this, and in the dark it might look enough like a real dinosaur to scare Chrissy Sue."

"Why wait until Pet Day?" Slap said. "It's dark right now, and the head's the only part she could see through a window." He grinned at Carlos.

Carlos grinned back. "Chrissy Sue might decide she believes in dinosaurs after all."

Slap yelled down the hall to his parents,

"We're going to the Danbys' house. We'll be back in just a little while."

"All right," his mother answered. "Be careful."

Lights were on in the Danbys' living room and kitchen. Mr. Danby and Jack were seated in the living room. Mr. Danby was talking, and Jack was scowling.

Slap and Carlos moved to the back of the house, where they could see through the large windows of the breakfast room into the kitchen. Mrs. Danby was making a cup of tea. Chrissy Sue was eating cookies from a box.

Her mother pointed to a plate. Chrissy Sue placed some cookies in a circle on the plate, but when her mother wasn't looking she popped another one in her mouth.

"It won't work," Carlos said. "We don't want to scare Mrs. Danby too."

"Shhh! Wait a minute," Slap said. Mrs. Danby left the kitchen carrying two cups of tea, but Chrissy Sue hung back, stuffing another cookie in her mouth.

"Now!" Slap said.

Carlos slipped the dragon head over his own, and Slap tapped at the window. Chrissy Sue,

who had picked up the plate of cookies, turned toward the window, startled.

As loudly as he could, Carlos roared and shoved the dragon's face toward the window.

Chrissy Sue screeched and dropped the plate. Cookies flew through the air.

"Run!" Carlos yelled, and took off as fast as he could go.

But Slap couldn't move. He hardly noticed Chrissy Sue jumping up and down and screaming. He stared at the objects on the Danbys' breakfast room table: a small key, a ring, and a coin.

Carlos ran back, grabbed Slap's arm, and tugged him away from the window. "Come on!" he whispered. "Do you want to get in trouble?"

Just then Slap heard Mr. Danby's voice. "It had to be your imagination," he said. "There are no dinosaurs in our backyard."

"Yes, there are, and it growled at me!" Chrissy Sue screeched.

"If you stop yelling, I'll go outside and look around," Slap heard her brother Jack say.

"Run!" Carlos said.

Slap ran. He didn't have to be reminded again.

6

When Carlos and Slap were safely inside Slap's bedroom, Slap threw himself across the bed, gasping until he could catch his breath.

"Did you see old Chrissy Sue's face?" Carlos began to laugh so hard he could hardly talk. "We really scared her! Those cookies! The way they went flying through the air! When you see Chrissy Sue at school Monday, tell her your dinosaur got loose!"

Carlos stopped laughing and looked at Slap. "What's the matter? Don't you think it was funny?" he asked.

Slap sat up and looked at Carlos. "Sure, it was a lot of fun scaring stupid old Chrissy Sue," he said. "I was just thinking about what I saw on her kitchen table."

"What did you see?" Carlos asked.

Quietly Slap answered, "A small key, a ring, and a coin."

Carlos's eyes grew wide. Then he said, "Oh, come on, Slap. You could find those things in anyone's house." He pointed at Slap's desk. "Look. You've got a small key right over there."

"It's a key to my coin bank," Slap said.

"There. You see. And you've got coins in your bank."

"No, I haven't," Slap said. "The bank's empty."

Carlos was still watching him, so even though Slap still had a funny feeling about what Chrissy Sue might be up to, he said, "You're right. I shouldn't suspect Chrissy Sue."

He began to smile as he remembered Chrissy Sue's face. "She sure did look funny when she screamed, didn't she?"

"Yeah! She better believe in your dinosaur now!"

"You looked pretty funny too, you know— especially when you were running across her lawn with that thing on your head and all the teeth flapping up and down."

"How'd you like the way I growled?"

Carlos roared loudly, and Slap growled back until Mrs. Slappey came in and told the boys she had a headache, and it was time to call it a night.

"Chrissy Sue won't give you any more trouble," Carlos said as he left, but Slap knew better. He knew Chrissy Sue. She wouldn't give up until she actually saw Slap with a dinosaur pet in hand. A real, live dinosaur.

Late that night Slap lay in bed unable to sleep. His sheet was pulled out at the bottom, and his blanket was twisted. Slap kicked at his blanket, but it only became more tangled.

Everyone else in his house was asleep, and Slap wished he could go to sleep, but he couldn't. He had to think of how to find a dinosaur for Pet Day.

As there were giant Komodo dragons on earth, maybe there were still a few *Apatosauruses* hanging around somewhere. Or just one *Tyrannosaurus Rex* hiding in a canyon. Or maybe one of those flying dinosaurs with the huge wings, a *pterodactyl*.

It would be nice to have a *pterodactyl*. She'd

swoop down on Chris's room and take all his footballs and basketballs and baseballs and soccer balls and carry them to her nest and try to hatch them. Wouldn't that make Chris mad! Slap smothered a laugh.

A Komodo dragon, on the other hand, would probably eat all the basketballs and soccer balls in one gulp.

Suddenly Slap got an idea. It was such a good idea he wondered why he hadn't thought of it right away. He sat up in bed and said aloud, "I know where I can get a dinosaur!"

His bedroom door opened, and his mother stepped into the room. "Are you all right, Slap?" she asked.

"I know where I can get a real, live dinosaur!" Slap told her.

His mother straightened his sheet and blanket. She helped him scoot down in bed and pulled the blanket up to his chin. Then she smoothed his hair away from his forehead. "You had a bad dream, dear," she said. "It's all right now. Just go back to sleep."

She tiptoed out of the room and quietly shut the door.

Slap closed his eyes, but he had a smile on his face. He hadn't had a bad dream. He'd had a good idea, and now he knew where he could find a dinosaur.

7

The next evening, around eight o'clock, Nikki telephoned. "My mother said she'd drive us to the pool right now," she said.

"Uh-oh," Slap said. "I forgot to ask if I could go."

"You forgot about the trap we're going to set? How could you?"

"I was thinking about dinosaurs," he told her.

Nikki made a strangling sound. "You and your dinosaurs," she muttered.

"Not dinosaurs. Just one. Dinosaur," Slap said.

"I don't want to talk about dinosaurs," Nikki

said. "Go ask your mother if you can go swimming. Right now."

"Your mother's not going to stay there with us, is she?" Slap asked. "Because if there are too many people around, the trap may not work."

"She won't stay," Nikki said. "She's just going to drop us off and come back and get us. The lifeguard will be there to watch us, and we can all swim, so she's not worried about us. Do you want to go, or don't you?"

"Yes, I do," Slap said. "Wait a second. I'll ask Mom." At the top of his lungs he yelled, "Mom!"

He heard a little whimper behind him. His mother was standing there holding her head. "Slap, I just came into the room," she said. "You don't have to shout."

"Oh," Slap said. "Sorry, Mom. Nikki's mother's going to drive the Nic-Nacs to the pool. We'll come home when it closes at nine. Okay? Can I go?"

"Yes," his mother said. "Just remember to thank Mrs. Kimble."

Slap wished his mother wouldn't always say things like that. Of course he'd remember.

"Okay!" he told Nikki. "I can come!"

Slap got into his swim suit and T-shirt as fast as he could and ran outside and down to Nikki's house, where the others were waiting.

When they arrived at the pool, Slap was the first one out of the car. As he ran ahead of the others toward the gate to the pool, one of his thongs flew off, frightening a squirrel, which dashed across his path.

The Nic-Nacs paused at the edge of the pool area. The swimming pool was more inviting in the sunlight with people laughing, shouting, and splashing. At this hour it was so quiet they could hear the quiet chatter and rustle of the pair of large black crows in the nearest elm tree. As Slap looked up, one of them swooped to a lower branch and stared at him.

"Caw, caw!" Slap said to the crow. The crow blinked, but it didn't look away.

"I bet the crows wish we'd turn off the lights so they could get to sleep," Slap said, but he was glad the lights were on.

It was dark beyond them, and for a moment Slap could imagine that the shadows were moving, crawling closer and closer.

The lifeguard sat alone on his tower, halfway down the side of the pool; and an elderly man swam silently back and forth, back and forth at the deep end. Slap gulped. They were here to try to set a trap, but what if someone did come out of the darkness to take the ring?

Someone . . . or some*thing*! In spite of the warm evening, Slap shivered.

"Our trap should work," Amy whispered. "We're practically the only ones here." She and Slap moved a little closer together.

Although all the tables were empty, Nikki put her ring on the same table it had been on the day before. Even in the shadows the glass stone flashed with the reflected lights from the pool.

"So what do we do now?" Amy asked.

"Go swimming," Carlos said. "That's what we're supposed to be doing here."

"We have to take turns keeping watch," Slap reminded him. "I'll take my turn first this time."

He sat under the tree, his towel wrapped around his shoulders, glancing now and then at the others, who were playing water tag. The ring remained on the table, a small spot of light in the near darkness.

Before long Amy ran up to him and stood dripping on his legs. "Your turn to swim," she

said, and Slap gladly shed his towel and shirt, ran to the pool, and jumped in.

When the lifeguard blew his whistle, Slap was surprised. Nine o'clock already?

As he climbed from the pool, he looked at the table. The ring was still there.

"Well, we tried," Nikki said.

Carlos finished toweling his hair and flipped one end of his towel at her legs.

"Ouch!" she cried, and twisted around, trying to flick her towel at Carlos.

Amy and Slap got into the game, shrieking and yelling and chasing each other around the tree.

"That's enough, kids!" the lifeguard shouted. He motioned to them from the gate. "Come on. Hurry up. I want to lock up and go home."

At that moment Nikki's mother drove into the parking lot, the headlights of her car sweeping across them.

"There's Mom!" Nikki said, and they raced out the gate and toward the car.

It took the lifeguard only a moment to pad-lock the gate, hop into his own car, and drive away.

But as the Nic-Nacs began to climb into Mrs.

Kimble's car, Slap stopped and said, "The ring! Nikki, did you get it?"

"Oh, no," she said. "I left it on the table."

Although there was no way to get through the locked gate, the Nic-Nacs ran to the chain-link fence to look at the table on which they'd left the ring.

Slap sucked in his breath. No one could have gotten inside the pool area after they had left, but the table was empty. The ring was gone!

He'd been kidding when he'd told the others that the swimming pool might be haunted. But what if he'd been right?

None of the Nic-Nacs had an answer to the mystery. Amy echoed Slap's own thoughts when she murmured, "Maybe there really is a ghost!"

Slap tried to sound brave. "I don't believe in ghosts," he said, but even though he tried as hard as he could, he wasn't able to come up with another answer.

8

In the morning it took extra time to feed Keetsy and clean his cage, so Slap had to run to get to school on time. When he staggered into the schoolyard, gasping to catch his breath, he heard someone yell, "There he is!"

He knew that voice. It was Chrissy Sue's voice.

"Hi, Slap," Chrissy Sue called. "Where's your dinosaur?"

The kids with Chrissy Sue laughed.

Carlos walked over to Slap and nudged him. "Tell her," he whispered.

Slap waited until Chrissy Sue and the others came closer. He tried to make his voice deep and mysterious as he said, "My dinosaur got loose Saturday night."

"It wandered around the neighborhood," Carlos said, "looking for someone—uh, something—to eat."

"Oh, sure," Chrissy Sue said.

"I heard it looked in your window," Slap said. "People could hear you screaming a mile away."

Chrissy Sue looked embarrassed, but she said, "You and Carlos were the ones who were scared! My brother, Jack, saw you running away with that dumb paper head. He said he never saw anybody run so fast."

"He saw the fastest dinosaur on earth," Carlos said.

"So that was your stupid dinosaur," Chrissy Sue said. "That's what you're going to bring to the park for Pet Day."

Slap shook his head. "Carlos and I were just having some fun with a paper head my brother, Chris, made," he told her. "That wasn't my dinosaur. Remember, I told you I'd bring a real, live dinosaur."

Chrissy Sue sneered. "You haven't got a dinosaur," she said.

"Yes, I do. Come to Pet Day and see him."

Chrissy Sue frowned. "It's not a *real* dinosaur," she said.

"Yes, it is," Slap said.

"It's not a *live* dinosaur," she added.

"Yes, it is," Slap said.

"You're making that up!" Chrissy Sue's face turned red.

Slap laughed and said, "No, I'm not."

"Liar, liar, pants on fire!" Chrissy Sue yelled.

Slap just grinned. "Wait until Pet Day," he said, and walked away.

Carlos caught up with him and said, "You can't keep saying you have a dinosaur, if you haven't got one."

"But I do have one," Slap said.

"You know you don't," Carlos said.

"I do so," Slap told him. "Wait until Pet Day. You'll see."

At lunchtime Nikki carried her tray to where Slap was sitting with Carlos in the school cafeteria. She put her tray on the table, spilling her vegetable soup into her tapioca pudding, and sat next to Slap.

"Slap, it's awful," Nikki murmured. "Everyone is talking and laughing about your dinosaur."

"That's not awful," Slap said.

"It is if you don't have a dinosaur," Nikki said.

"But it isn't, because I do," Slap told her.

As Slap came back to the classroom after lunch, Mrs. Lambkin smiled and motioned to him to come to her desk. "One of your neighbors—Mr. Wallace—is a friend of mine, and he gave me a copy of your neighborhood newspaper. I like what you wrote about the *Nanotyrannus*."

Some of the kids were listening. Slap was glad. "Thanks," he said. "I'd like to do my science report about the *Nanotyrannus*."

"That's a good idea," she told him. "Maybe the dinosaur you're making could be a part of your report."

"I'm not making a dinosaur," he said.

Mrs. Lambkin looked puzzled. "Oh," she said. "I thought I heard that you were making a paper dinosaur for Pet Day at the park."

Slap shook his head. Everyone in the class was quiet. They were all listening. Slap tried very hard not to laugh. "Somebody has been starting rumors," he said as he stared at Chrissy Sue. "My brother made a paper dinosaur head.

Ask Chrissy Sue how loud she screamed when she saw it."

Chrissy Sue stuck out her tongue, but Slap ignored her. "I *am* bringing a dinosaur to Pet Day, but it's not paper. It's a real, live dinosaur."

Mrs. Lambkin studied him for a moment. Then she smiled. "I understand," she said. "You want it to be a surprise."

She stood up and opened a book. "All right, class," she announced. "We're going to work on our spelling."

After school Amy said to Slap, "This whole thing about your dinosaur is going to be a big joke. Right?"

"My dinosaur isn't a big joke," Slap said.

"But you don't really have a dinosaur," Amy said.

"Yes, I do," Slap said.

He walked home with Carlos.

"What are you going to do when Pet Day comes?" Carlos asked.

"Bring my dinosaur."

"I mean *really*," Carlos said.

"I'll really bring my dinosaur," Slap said.

Carlos shrugged. "Okay," he said. "Have it

your way. Do you want to come over after we do our homework?"

"Sure," Slap said. "But don't ask any more questions about my dinosaur. Okay?"

"Okay," Carlos said.

During the week the Nic-Nacs didn't mention Slap's dinosaur, but at school the other kids teased him about it.

"Do you have a leash for your dinosaur?" Chrissy Sue asked him. She giggled and poked Laura Lee Boswell, who sat next to Chrissy Sue. Laura Lee giggled too.

"I hope you feed your dinosaur before you bring him to the park," Jeff Allen said, and nearly fell down laughing.

"Maybe we should call Channel Two, so they can get a film crew there," Sally Parker told Slap. "People would like to see a real, live dinosaur on the TV news."

But no matter what anyone said, Slap just smiled. "You'll see my dinosaur on Saturday," he said.

Slap could hardly wait for Saturday to come.

9

On Saturday morning the Nic-Nacs met in Nikki's backyard.

"I gave Izzy a bath last night," Carlos said. "I want him to look his best."

"I painted a box to carry Speedy in," Nikki said.

"Mom gave me a beautiful blue ribbon and bow to put around Cinderella's neck," Amy said. "It matches one of her eyes."

"Wait until you see my dinosaur," Slap said. He grinned.

Nikki rolled her eyes. "You and your big secrets," she said.

On Saturday afternoon Slap ran all the way to

Mrs. January's house. He ran so fast he scared some crows that were hunting for bugs. They flew up to a tree branch cawing loudly.

"Caw, caw!" Slap yelled at them, and gave a couple of leaps into the air. He felt great.

Slap dashed up the steps, unlocked the front door, and unhooked Keetsy's cage from its stand. "You and I are going to the park," he said.

As Slap carried Keetsy outside and down the steps to the sidewalk, Nikki came out of her house. She was carrying a red-and-blue box very carefully.

She saw Slap and called, "Wait for me." When she caught up with him, she looked at Keetsy and asked, "What are you doing with Keetsy?"

"I'm taking him to the park for Pet Day," Slap said.

Nikki looked disappointed. "You said you were going to bring a dinosaur," she reminded him.

Slap tried hard not to laugh. "He'll be there," he promised.

"Oh, sure," Nikki said. "If you have a dinosaur, then where is he?"

"Hurry up," Slap said. "Let's go to the park, or we're going to be late."

"You're not going to tell me?"

"I'm going to surprise you," Slap said.

"You and your surprises," Nikki said.

Amy, who was carrying Cinderella, joined them, and Carlos yelled for them to wait. Tony was with Carlos, helping to hold Izzy's leash.

Tony wanted to see all the pets. He put his face against Keetsy's cage. "Hello, Keetsy," Tony said.

Slap made a tiny, high voice, trying to sound like a bird. "Hello, Tony," he said.

But Tony saw Slap's lips move, and he thought that was very funny. He stroked Cinderella and patted Speedy. He liked to watch Speedy pull his head into his shell and poke it out again.

When Tony was ready Carlos took his hand, and the Nic-Nacs walked to the park together.

A crowd of kids had already arrived, and pets were everywhere. There were a lot of dogs, big, little, and middle size; and they all seemed to be making noise. The pair of crows that nested in the trees near the swimming pool swooped overhead, cawing loudly as they scolded everyone for disturbing their peace.

Pete yelled for everybody to get in line, and finally they did. A lot of the kids looked at Slap and Keetsy. Some of them whispered to each other. A few of them snickered.

Slap didn't care. He just stood in line, holding Keetsy's bird cage.

Chrissy Sue sauntered up to Slap. Slap reached out and patted her puppy. Snuggles licked his hand.

"Liar, liar," Chrissy Sue said. "You told us you'd bring a dinosaur."

"I did," Slap said.

"Ha-ha," Chrissy Sue said. "Then where is he?"

"Wait and see," Slap told her.

Chrissy Sue stepped on Slap's toes as she walked past him to get to the head of the line.

A parade was first on Pete's schedule. One cat ran away, and two kids fell over their dogs. *Other than that*, Slap thought, *it was a pretty good parade.*

Next Pete asked the kids, in turn, to show off their pets. Some of the dogs did tricks.

As each pet was shown, Pete gave it an award certificate. There was one for biggest pet, funniest pet, and fattest pet. Pete had made enough awards so that every pet got one. Carlos let Tony hold Izzy's award.

Finally it was Slap's turn. He held up Keetsy's cage and said, "This is my dinosaur."

Some of the kids laughed and hooted, but Slap said, "Give me a chance, and I'll explain."

When Pete had made everyone quiet down, Slap told them what the scientists had discovered. He held up Keetsy's cage. "Birds' ankles are like *Tyrannosaurus* ankles," Slap said, "and scientists think the hip bones and knee bones are the same."

Keetsy took two steps sideways on his perch. He knew Slap was talking about him.

"And even the back and the ribs and the neck are alike," Slap said. "And the tyrannosaurs' arms would look like the bones in birds' wings if their arms were longer."

Most of the kids were interested and were listening, but Chrissy Sue scowled. "So what?" she said.

"There's more," Slap said. "The *Nanotyrannus* skull has air passages to cool the brain, just like birds' skulls have."

Pete said, "I read that article too, about birds being descendants of dinosaurs."

"That means birds really are dinosaurs," Amy said.

"Real, live dinosaurs," Carlos said.

Nikki glared at Chrissy Sue. "We all agree to that," she said.

Pete held up a hand. "Just a minute. What Slap told us is interesting, but remember that it's only a theory," he said.

Chrissy Sue smirked. She opened her mouth to say something, but Slap spoke first.

"Lots of things we have proof for started out as theories," Slap said. "Once it was only a theory that the world was round."

"Okay," Pete said with a smile. "I'll buy that." He held up one of the awards, but Chrissy Sue stepped forward.

"Slap shouldn't get an award," she said. When the Nic-Nacs began to protest, she hurried to say, "I'm not talking about dumb dinosaur birds. I'm talking about pets. We were supposed to bring our own pets, and Slap brought Mrs. January's."

"The parakeet's not yours?" Pete asked Slap.

"Yes, he is mine," Slap answered. "Mrs. January said Keetsy would be *my* pet while she was away visiting her relatives, and she hasn't come back to Houston yet, so he's still mine."

Nikki spoke up. "That's exactly what Mrs. January said. I heard her."

Pete nodded. "We can't argue with that," he said. "As far as I'm concerned, Keetsy is Slap's pet today, and today's the day I'm giving out awards." He held up an award certificate. "I think Slap should get the prize for most unusual pet," he said. "And I hope there's a story about all this in the next issue of *The Nic-Nac News.*"

But Slap didn't step back. He said to Pete, "I think I solved the mystery of the things that disappeared around the swimming pool too. A dinosaur took them."

Some of the kids groaned, some hooted, and Chrissy Sue shouted, "Oh, no! Not again!" Even Pete looked surprised.

"I mean it," Slap said. "It may take some tree-climbing to find out, but I think I'm right. I forgot how much crows like bright, shiny objects. I bet the missing things are in their nest."

Nikki laughed. "And crows are dinosaurs too! Slap, you're terrific! You have to be right! You solved the mystery!"

"I don't think he's so terrific," Chrissy Sue said. "I knew the answer all along, only I didn't say so because nobody asked me."

Slap leaned close enough so that only Chrissy Sue could hear him. "Grasshopper guts!" he said.

When Slap got home, his father and Chris were outside in the backyard practicing hoop shots with a basketball, so Slap showed his award to his mother and told her the same things about dinosaurs that he'd said in the park.

"I'm proud of you, Slap. You do so many interesting things," his mother said.

For a moment Slap felt good, but he glanced out the back window where Chris had just tried for a slam dunk. "But I'm not good at sports," Slap said.

His mother put an arm around his shoulders and stood with him watching Chris make another basket. "Chris thinks he'll never be able to match your abilities in science," she said.

"Really?" Slap was surprised. It had never occurred to him that he could be better than his big brother in something.

Now he really felt great. "If there's enough

time before dinner," he said, "maybe I'll make a frame for my award. Or maybe I'll draw a dinosaur chart for my science project at school."

He grinned at his mother. "I know," he said. "What I'd better do first is write about who won the awards at Pet Day for *The Nic-Nac News*."